Joan's Tea Time

by Liza Charlesworth

ISBN: 978-1-338-84447-4

Art Director: Tannaz Fassihi; Designer: Cynthia Ng; Illustrated by Michael Robertson
Copyright © Liza Charlesworth. All rights reserved. Published by Scholastic Inc.

2 3 4 5 68 26 25 24

Printed in Jiaxing, China. First printing, June 2022.

■SCHOLASTIC

See Joan.
Joan is a nice gal.

"My pal Peet can meet
for tea at five," says Joan.

Joan can clean up her home
to make it neat.

Joan can make a fine cake.
Bake, bake, bake!

Joan can make
a big pot of tea.

Joan can make
a big pile of seeds.

6

Joan can place
a big rose in a vase.

Joan can seat Toad and Ape.
They will not make a peep.

It is five.
Is Joan set for tea? Yes!

So Joan says, "Peet, Peet!
It is time to meet for tea."

See Peet.
Peet is a nice bird.
Peet is cute. Peet is huge!

11

Joan can sip tea.
Peet can eat seeds
with his beak.

Sip, sip. Eat, eat.
"I like tea time!" says Joan.
"I like tea time!" says Peet.

Read & Review

Invite your learner to point to each long-vowel word and read it aloud.

i_e
pile
fine
nice
five
time
like

a_e
vase
bake
ape
cake
make
place

o_e
home
rose

u_e
huge
cute

ea
neat
eat
beak
clean
tea
seat

ee
meet
see
peep
Peet
seeds

oa
Joan
toad

15

Fun Fill-Ins

Read the sentences aloud, inviting your learner to complete them using the long-vowel words in the box.

> Joan   cake   tea   five   huge

1. The name of the girl is _____.

2. Tea time is at _____.

3. Joan bakes a fine _____.

4. Peet is cute and very _____.

5. At the end, Gail

   sips _____.